SQUABBLES

Written by Stephen Cosgrove
Illustrated by Robin James

A Serendipity™ *Book*

PSS!
PRICE STERN SLOAN

Dedicated to battered people everywhere,
may you learn to fear no more.

— Stephen

Farther than far, in the middle of the Crystal Sea, is a magical island called Serendipity. Deep in the forests of Serendipity, where everything is crisp and cool, is a place called Forest Glade. Well-worn shady paths wind through the trees like gentle boulevards in a city of tall buildings. Golden leaves, tired from clinging to their places in the sun, spin silently to the path below.

Things are ordered and organized here in the Forest Glade. Even the wild flowers don't truly grow wild; instead, they are neatly planted in hanging baskets of woven wheat, straw, and vine.

The Pristine Path, bordered in flowers of quiet colors, was a meeting place for the creatures that lived in Forest Glade. Here, squirrel met rabbit met possum, as they moved on their way doing one chore or another. Along the way, they would politely inquire of the weather or whether it was time to pluck the fruits from the tree.

If you looked off the path, you would notice neighborhoods of sorts: dens, burrows, and nested limb where all the creatures lived. All was quiet here, from the muted laughter of children playing to the wistful whispers of neighbor gossiping to neighbor.

One day in early fall, a new family moved to Forest Glade—a family of raccoons called the Squabbles: Momma and Poppa Squabble and a boy called Junior.

They appeared normal in all respects, but there was something amiss, something not quite right. There was a wildness in the eyes of Poppa and a bit of fear, if you like, in the eyes of Momma and Junior.

They set up housekeeping in an old hollowed stump that sat at the edge of the Pristine Path. Here, the Squabble family unpacked their things and here, they thought they would always stay.

Junior scampered to the very top of the stump and looked about, nose twitching excitedly in the air. In the meantime, Momma Squabble bustled busily about her new home as Poppa pulled some weeds that seemed out of place in this ordered land.

As was the custom in Forest Glade, a few of the creatures that had lived there for some time stopped and wished Poppa Squabble welcome. Poppa stopped his chores, and stood with the creatures at the edge of the path, passing the time with idle chat.

From inside the stump came the gentle whines of Junior begging Momma to be allowed to run where the other forest children ran. Momma said, "No. I'm afraid it's a little too late to be exploring." To which Junior cried, "But Momma, the other kids are still playing."

Poppa Squabble patiently ignored the ruckus at first. Then as he tried to concentrate on his conversation, he finally said, "Excuse me for just a moment." He turned to the stump and screamed at the top of his lungs, "Shut up! Our neighbors have no need of the Squabbles's squabbles." Then, as if nothing had happened, he turned back to the shocked creatures on the path and rejoined the conversation.

Among the other creatures who lived in Forest Glade, there was a bright young bunny called Buttermilk who became Junior's best friend. The two of them would scamper about playing nose tag or hide-and-go-sneak. For days and days they had played together just like all other creatures in the forest.

But one morning, Junior was late for play and when he came his tail was dragging and a tear refused to dry in his eye. Buttermilk rushed to her friend and asked, "What's the matter? Why are you late?"

Junior brushed the tear from his eye and said sullenly, "Nothing's the matter. I'm late because. . . I, uh . . . fell out of bed. And I'm crying because it hurts."

Sure enough, Buttermilk could see welts and bruises all over the little raccoon's cheek and arms that could have happened if someone fell hard from bed.

Later that afternoon, Buttermilk walked with Junior back to his home off the Pristine Path and was invited in by Momma Squabble. "Buttermilk," Junior's mother said, "would you care for some cookies and milk?"

"Yes, thank you," answered Buttermilk politely. She grinned at Junior who made a face at her as they waited for their afternoon treat. As the mother raccoon bustled about, Buttermilk noticed that Momma Squabble had bruises and bumps on her cheeks and arms, too, and her eye was black as a boot heel. "Gee whiz, Mrs. Squabbles," gushed Buttermilk, "did you fall out of bed too?"

Momma Squabble shot a curious look at Junior who stared into his glass of milk, "Yes, yes, Buttermilk," she flustered as she nervously touched hand to cheek. "I fell out of bed, too."

Buttermilk didn't think anything more about it until later that night as the stars began to explode in a purple crystal sky. She was hurrying home from an errand when she heard crashing and banging coming from inside the stump where the Squabbles lived. She stopped for a moment, curious about the noise and then heard bellowing and yelling like she had never heard before. She stood there at the edge of the path afraid to move and afraid not to.

For the voice that was yelling was none other than Poppa Squabble himself. He shouted that everything was wrong—from Momma's dinner to Junior's chores. His bellowing was softened only by Momma Squabble as she urged him, begged him, not to get mad.

"Don't get mad?" he shouted. "You are telling me not to get mad?" Softer now and yet more threatening Poppa Squabble continued, "Well, little woman, I'm not going to get mad. . . I am going to get the belt."

Through the open window Buttermilk could see him storm from the room. Her stomach was aching but she didn't know why. Tears welled in her eyes as she watched her friend and his mother cower in their own home. Buttermilk could watch no more. She rushed home as a single, stifled cry echoed from the home of the Squabbles into the stillness of the night.

The little rabbit burst into the house and into her father's arms. "My, my," he said, "why the tears, my little Buttermilk Bunny?"

"Oh, daddy," she cried, "I just saw and heard the most horrible things and I don't know what to do!"

Her father picked her up and said, "There's nothing so horrible, seen nor heard, that you can't tell me or your mother."

With that, Buttermilk told him of the bumps and bruises she had seen that morning and all that she had just seen outside the stump.

Leaving Buttermilk at home, her father rushed down the path to where the Squabbles lived. There, he was joined by others of the glade who had heard all the goings on. Sure enough, inside the stump, through the window opened wide, was Poppa Squabble threatening Momma and Junior with a belt.

All the creatures on the path quickly huddled together. "What should we do?" they asked one another. "Should we knock on the door and see what we can do?"

"It is spoken," said one, "that all creatures have a right to privacy in their own home."

"Yes," whispered Buttermilk's father through clenched teeth, "but not when they are beating those smaller than themselves. No one has that right."

They moved as one to the door and with furry fists they rapped. The yelling stopped inside and all was quiet. Slowly the door opened and there stood Poppa Squabble, the belt still held in his hand. "What do you want?" he gruffly asked.

"We want," said Buttermilk's father, "for you to stop beating your wife and child."

"Harrumph," puffed Poppa Squabble, "they are mine and I will do with them as I please." With that he began to close the door.

"No," said the elder rabbit firmly. "They are not yours to own and do with as you please, for they have rights, too." Boldly, he reached out and grabbed Poppa Squabbles firmly by the arm and led him from the stump as the others consoled the mother and her child.

By the next day, things had settled down in Forest Glade, but few had forgotten nor ever would.

Poppa Squabble really loved his family but just couldn't control his anger. For a while he lived apart, but in that time he learned that a family is not a possession. He learned not to strike others in anger. But most of all he learned that forgiveness can be earned only by deed.

AS YOU LOOK AROUND AT FRIENDS
WHETHER BUNNY, SQUIRREL OR OTHER,
DON'T BE AFRAID TO INTERFERE
FOR WE ARE EACH OTHER'S BROTHER.

Serendipity™ Books

Created by
Stephen Cosgrove and Robin James

Enjoy all the delightful books in the Serendipity™ Series:

Available wherever books are sold.

PSS!
PRICE STERN SLOAN